Rachel Jane Fearnley, Harriet Ann Fearnley

Crumbs from the Master's Table

Rachel Jane Fearnley, Harriet Ann Fearnley

Crumbs from the Master's Table

ISBN/EAN: 9783744746861

Printed in Europe, USA, Canada, Australia, Japan

Cover: Foto ©Andreas Hilbeck / pixelio.de

More available books at **www.hansebooks.com**

CRUMBS

MASTER'S TABLE.

BY

RACHEL JANE AND HARRIET ANN FEARNLEY.

For our Saviour's sake.

PRINTED BY T. BREAR & CO., LIMITED, BRADFORD.
FOR PRIVATE CIRCULATION.
1899.

INTRODUCTION.

Sister and I have just passed another birthday anniversary, and it is wonderful when we look back on the past years of our lives to think of all the way in which God has led us. We praise Him for having given to us good parents, who have striven, ever since we can remember, to train us up in paths of truth and grace, and it is no doubt through their training and example, backed by God's grace and blessing, that we are what we are to-day. We were taken by them to the Sanctuary, and sent early to the Sabbath-school, and through the holy influences associated with these blessed places, along with home influences, sister and I were led to give our hearts to God when we were very young, for which we are very glad. We have had many and varied experiences during our Christian lives, having had both cloud and sunshine ; but our greatest regret is that we have not lived nearer to God. We have been unable for some time now to join in much active service in the Church or Sunday-school owing to nervous debility and weakness, which has tended to bar us from even attending our chapel as we otherwise would have done. But God ofttimes visited us in our quiet moments, and has given to us thoughts and feelings which have tended, when we were deprived of meeting with His people, to give us comfort and draw us nearer to Himself; and through God's help we have been able to write down a few of these, which we hope will be blessed to the comforting and helping of many of our brothers and sisters in Christ, and may God bless them to the converting of many who have not yet given their hearts to Him is our desire.

POEMS.

Text—" *Choose ye this day whom ye will serve.*"

In springtide's early morning,
　　Before the opening day,
Two youths commenced life's journey,
　　They can no longer stay.

Their hopes are strong and buoyant,
　　Their aims are large and high,
And they are both determined
　　To dwell beyond the sky.

They find life's morn a garden,
　　All decked with springtide's flowers,
With pleasant fountains flowing
　　'Mid fragrant shady bowers.

So on they go together,
　　And travel hand in hand,
As in their minds they picture
　　Some happy Eden-land.

Thither their steps shall lead them,
　　And fancy says good speed ;
They want a hand to guide them
　　And soon they feel their need.

They feel this earth shall perish
　　With all its glittering scenes,
But truth and right shall flourish
　　As never failing streams.

And here a voice says to them,
  Choose now the way you'll take,
Whether to scoff and scorn me
  Or suffer for my sake.

For they who would gain heaven
  Must now themselves deny,
And on God's Word as given,
  They must in faith rely.

The end of this is glory,
  And yieldeth great reward,
For those who with Christ suffer
  Shall there adore their Lord.

So let us now press forward
  To that bright heaven above,
Knowing that all we meet with
  Is sent to us in love.

To make us still more like Him,
  E're He shall bid us go,
To mansions there provided
  For all His saints below.

By R. J. FEARNLEY.

Text—"*Ere the cock crow twice thou shalt deny
    Me thrice.*"

SEE my loving gracious Saviour,
  In the Judgment Hall He stands,
He is there reproached and hated,
  Bearing blows from cruel hands.

In my place He stands before them,
  For my sins He pays the price,
And by me who saw and knew Him
  He is there denied thrice.

Still He looks in grief and pity
   On His weak and erring one,
And His look means true forgiveness,
   For it breaks the heart of stone.

Now He is led forth to Calvary,
   There to bear my sin and shame,
So that I through His atonement
   Might have everlasting gain.

And Thou hasted from high Heaven
   All my sins and griefs to bear,
So that to me might be given
   A sweet place of resting there.

Help me, Saviour, to accept Thee
   Now with all my mind and heart,
So I shall with all Thy loved ones
   Bear an everlasting part.

               By R. J. FEARNLEY

Text—" He has now led captivity captive."

OUR dear Saviour Christ is risen
   On this gladsome Easter morn,
And we would with richest laurels
   His dear conquering brow adorn.

He is worthy of all power,
   Here on earth and high in heaven,
In this happy sacred hour   .
   From each heart all praise be given.

For the hope which He has brought us
   Of a glorious future bliss,
Which we shall enjoy forever,
   Having run our course in this.

We shall there in joy adore Him,
　　Evermore beyond the skies,
We shall sing and bow before Him,
　　Who for us hath won the prize.

We shall through His spirit conquer
　　All the powers of death and hell,
And we shall through God, our Father,
　　Hear the words, Thou hast done well.

Help us, oh our heavenly Father,
　　Through our Saviour to o'ercome,
Until Thou in love shalt gather
　　All Thy wandering children home.

Then we will rejoice in glory,
　　Bless and praise the Holy Name
Of the Lamb of God forever,
　　For to save our souls He came.

　　　　　　　By R. J. FEARNLEY.

Text—" All things praise Thee."

SWEET Spring has dawned upon us,
　　In shades of richest green,
While Nature's sweetest flowers
　　In loveliest tints are seen.

We feel that all around us
　　Is bidding us rejoice ;
With notes of sweetest music
　　We hear their gladsome voice.

All Nature's now reviving,
　　The joyful sunny hours
Are with each other striving,
　　With all their God-given powers.

The sweet refreshing showers
  Which God gives from the sky,
Remind us of rich treasures
  Laid up for us on high.

The most delightful pictures
  Which now come to our sight,
Are not to be compared
  To things in heaven's clear light.

There is life's flowing river,
  Who's ever tranquil stream
Glides on, where joys forever
  In rich abundance teem.

There we shall be with Jesus,
  Our loving Lord who came
To save each soul who trusts Him,
  Believing in His name.

Oh let my life like springtime
  Yield fruits of praise to Thee,
So shall I, when in heaven,
  Thy richer glory see.

By R. J. FEARNLEY.

*Text—" I had rather be a doorkeeper in the house of
God than dwell in tents of wickedness."*

I FEEL, dear Lord, 'tis good to go
  Into Thy courts while here below,
It does indeed my soul o'erpower
  While thinking of that blissful hour

When I shall stand in Thee complete,
  And fitted for that blissful seat,
Which Thou hast in Thy boundless love
  Fit up for me in courts above.

Thou did'st in love mark out my way,
  Right from this earth to realms of day ;
There thou hast treasured up for me
  Rare joys which I shall one day see.

For Thou hast promised there to bring
  The soul that is redeemed from sin,
And every soul that trusts in Thee
  Shall from all sin and shame be free.

Be mine, O Lord, this better part,
  That with clean hands and upright heart
I may in that day reign with Thee
  Throughout a blest eternity.

And may I with sweet patience run
  My earthly course till it be done,
And I shall then for ever share
  In untold heights of glory there.

Let me now reckon all things loss,
  And gladly here endure the cross,
With my dear Saviour there to reign
  Secure from sin and death and pain.

So I shall through Thee conquer all,
  And ready hearken for Thy call,
For Thou wilt soon receive Thine own
  And give them each a golden crown.

By R. J. FEARNLEY.

Text—" He is faithful who hath promised."

As Thou didst to ancient Israel
  All Thy promises perform,
So Thou hast to all Thy children
  Proved a refuge from the storm.

Thou hast given to us a Saviour,
 As our surety He doth stand ;
He's the rock of our salvation,
 He will lead us by the hand.

Help us, Father, to accept Him,
 In this solemn, sacred hour,
And with purpose cleave unto Him,
 He will give us strength and power

To pursue our heavenward journey,
 As along life's path we go,
Feeling He is close beside us,
 He will bring us safely through,

To that Eden land of promise,
 New Jerusalem above,
Where the souls of all who serve Him
 Shall be brought through His great love.

Those who pass through tribulation,
 Walking through dark vales below,
They shall find Him their salvation,
 As from earth to heaven they go.

So, our loving Heavenly Father,
 We would ever trust in Thee,
Knowing that Thine hand is mighty,
 Thou art He who holds the key.

We are poor and weak and erring,
 We cannot Thy ways explain,
But we trust to Thy great wisdom,
 Thou wilt make the crooked plain.

Thus we go, on Thee relying,
 In full hope of glory rest,
Trusting that our souls when dying
 Shall be found of Heaven possessed.

     By R. J. FEARNLEY.

Text—" My heart's desire."

Oh let Thy Holy Spirit, Lord,
  Take full possession of my heart :
Oh may I through Thy gracious word
  Be fully freed from sin's sad smart.

Oh let me closer walk with Thee,
  And have Thy presence all the way,
So shall this life a heaven be
  Leading to one eternal day.

I shall through Thee life's journey run,
  And gain the victory through Thy strength ;
Oh may I hear Thee say well done,
  So I shall reign with Thee at length.

Oh let my fading vision see
  Life's sun set in a tranquil sky,
So shall I ever be with Thee,
  With happy spirits up on high.

                              By R. J. FEARNLEY.

Text—" Whosoever believeth in Him shall be saved."

Our Gracious Saviour, Jesus Christ,
  The Lord of earth and heaven,
Unto each soul that trusts in Him
  He hath the assurance given.

In childhood's paths he took my hand
  In tenderness and love,
He gave me views of that bright land
  Prepared for me above.

Where all the ransomed white-robed throng
  Shall gather in one band,
To join the everlasting song
  And sit at His right hand.

And though we meet with trials here,
  Which tries the wounded heart,
It does our drooping spirits cheer
  To know He takes our part.

He too while dwelling here below
  Did all our sorrows share,
Along the path He travelled through
  He carried all our care.

He loved the mourning heart to cheer,
  With tender words and kind ;
He did give hearing to the deaf,
  And seeing to the blind.

And to the heart by sin oppressed
  He spake sweet words of peace,
Bidding us come to Him for rest,
  And from His bounties feast.

Help me, dear Saviour, to be Thine,
  And suffer for Thy sake ;
Oh fill my heart with love divine,
  And then to heaven take.

                    By R. J. FEARNLEY.

Text—" The Lord is at our right hand."

Oh, gracious Saviour, loving Lord,
  Thou seest all our grief ;
According to Thy precious word,
  Come now to our relief.

Thou seest us as we prostrate wait,
  Helpless and weak and sad ;
Thou bidst us stay, nor leave Thy gate,
  And Thou wilt make us glad.

Thou know'st the ardent strong desire
  Of every longing heart :
We pray that with Thy holy fire
  Thou wilt inspire each heart.

And though we feel at times depressed
  With weakness, doubt, and fear,
Help us in faith on Thee to rest
  And Thou wilt dry each tear.

Help us, while reading Thy sweet word,
  To clearly see our way,
And may we grow more like our Lord
  Through each succeeding day.

Help us, dear Lord, with holy zeal
  To cling with fervent heart
To Thee, and ever do Thy will,
  Nor from Thy ways depart.

                    By R. J. FEARNLEY.

IN REMEMBRANCE OF THE LONG REIGN OF QUEEN VICTORIA.

(IN JUBILEE YEAR.)

IT is with deep affection
  I now pourtray the scene,
Which comes from sweet reflection
  On your long reign as queen.
What blessings God has given
  Unto this favoured land,
And though great foes have striven,
  He's strengthened our right hand.
What peace and heavenly blessing
  Your Majesty hath seen,
God's grace and love possessing,
  Through your long reign our queen.

We still would pray God's favour
  Upon your head to rest,
That care or fear may never
  Your peace on earth molest.
And may your noble station
  A beacon light be seen,
And may each tribe and nation
  Say "God bless England's queen."
Thus living in God's favour,
  Through life's great work below,
We shall in bliss for ever
  God's lasting favour know.
And may the glorious record
  Of your long reign below
Never know strife or discord,
  As on through life you go;
Oh, may each loyal subject
  Ever be true in heart,
God's love our highest object,
  We still shall take our part.
For truth and men's salvation,
  We still shall pray and fight,
While this our favoured nation
  Trust God, and do the right.
Oh, may pure joy in heaven,
  And glory yet unseen,
By our dear Lord be given
  To you our favoured queen.

           By R. J. FEARNLEY.

IN MEMORY OF OUR SWEET LITTLE BIRD.

'Tis to our sweet little songster
  I would these few lines subscribe,
He was such a charming fellow,
  Quite the dearest of his tribe.

He would chant in happy measure,
  Making every heart rejoice,

And we felt him such a treasure,
　He had such a soft, sweet voice.

When the heart felt sad and weary,
　He would chant in sweetest lays,
Causing all that's sad and dreary
　Thus to yield to sunny rays.

There had such a winning carol
　To our little bird been given,
Which would lead the happy spirits
　Right way from earth to heaven.

Thus our gracious Heavenly Father
　Gives us messengers of love,
By their sweet rich voice to draw us
　From this earth to realms above.

How those precious little songsters
　Cause our hearts in faith and love
To ascend in joyous transport
　To the highest heaven above.

Help me, Lord, in happy measure,
　My dear Saviour to adore ;
He is my sole help and treasure,
　I would love Him more and more.

　　　　　　By R. J. FEARNLEY.

*Text—" He hath borne our sins and carried our
　　　　sorrows."*

HATH not all the prophet's words
Been in truth fulfilled ?
Truly, Lord, Thy bitter cup
To the brim wast filled.
Thou didst live a lowly life
For the sinner's sake,

From its heaviest load of strife
Thou didst daily take.
We would adore and daily praise
Thy loving words and gentle ways.

Thou, dear Saviour, too hast borne
From proud lips which saith :
" Can there any good thing come
Out of Nazareth ?"
'Mid the cruel scoffers' sneers,
Which at Thee were cast,
Thou hast dried the mourner's tears
And hast calmed the blast.
We would adore and daily praise
Thy loving words and gentle ways.

Thou didst in the garden pray
In deep agony :
" Oh my Father, take away
This great load from me.
Not as I will, oh my God,
I would ever say,
Help me now to bear the rod,
And Thy word obey ;"
We would adore and daily praise
Thy loving words and gentle ways.

Thou hast died on Calvary,
Suffered for my soul,
Thou hast fully ransomed me,
Saying, " Be thou whole."
Help me, Lord, to worship Thee,
And take up each cross,
Knowing what I bear for Thee
Never shall be loss,
We would adore and daily praise
Thy loving words and gentle ways.

By R. J. FEARNLEY.

B

*Text—"I said I will take heed to my ways that I sin
        not with my tongue."*

THE man who can control his heart,
    And guard his tongue where'er he go,
Is playing the true warrior's part,
    Which doth o'ercome his greatest foe.

How oft is scattered deadly seed,
    Which fills some other heart with pain,
And thus their path is strewn with weed
    Instead of rich and golden grain.

Sharper than lance or cutting sword,
    As arrows when unguarded slung,
Thus one unruly thoughtless word,
    As keenest fire from Satan flung.

But oh how good to say even less,
    If I but take another's part,
Striving to comfort, cheer, and bless,
    Showing a meek and loving heart,

I shall have peace and joy even here,
    Striving to bless I shall be blest ;
My heart shall find sweet comfort here,
    With hope of an eternal rest.

So may my voice sweet music make,
    To cheer and comfort all around ;
If I do this for Jesus's sake,
    His blessing shall my life surround.

I shall not thus have lived in vain,
    Or scattered discord in my way ;
But what I sow shall yield rich gain,
    I hear my loving Saviour say.

Eye hath not seen, nor ear hath heard,
   What is laid up for us above,
If we according to God's word
   Live a pure life of peace and love.

                By R. J. FEARNLEY.

Text—" Abraham's faith was counted to him for
*   righteousness."*

IT was not well that we,
   The creatures of a day,
Should have our best affections set
   On things which fleet away.

Could we have all things here
   According to our will,
The things which charm our vision most
   Would prove our greatest ill.

Thy faithful saint of old,
   Who chose Thee as his Lord,
Was glad to pitch his tent below
   According to Thy word.

And to commune with Thee,
   He built an altar there,
Where, in true reverence, faith, and love,
   He breathed his fervent prayer.

And Thou in love drew near
   The faithful soul to bless,
With promises so rich and rare,
   Which did his joy increase.

Thus did Thy servant go,
   Trusting in Thee alone :
Waiting for that eternal bliss
   When he the race had run.

So all Thy children trust
  In Thy great love and skill,
Which shall our every step direct,
  If we but do Thy will.

> By R. J. FEARNLEY.

Text—"*I am the Good Shepherd; My sheep hear
  My voice.*"

WHEN my soul was well-nigh sinking
  Under waves of deep distress,
I have heard the voice of Jesus,
  Which has caused the storm to cease.

He has come unto my rescue,
  Knowing I am weak and frail,
He has brought His grace to help me,
  Seeing I should surely fail.

When my heart has been elated
  With bright prospects I could see,
Christ has come and gently told me
  "Satan fain would conquer thee."

He has known my greatest failing,
  When I felt so firm and bold,
How in doubt and tribulation
  I should need faith's strongest hold.

How I should be tried like Peter,
  In that dreadful Judgment Hall,
Having with dark foes to struggle
  Until I for mercy call.

Jesus sees my heart's intention,
  How I fain would fight for Him,
How the world and its allurements
  Fain would strive my heart to win.

He is ever close beside me,
  He will strengthen my right hand,
And will guide me safe to glory,
  To that blessed, happy land.

There shall end life's care and trial,
  And my pilgrimage shall cease ;
I shall ever be with Jesus
  In that land of joy and peace.

By R. J. Fearnley.

CHRISTMAS DAY, 1896.

On this gladsome Christmas morning,
  Which reminds us of Christ's birth,
We with joy would hail the dawning
  Of our day-star upon earth :
We would hail the sign thus given
Of our dear Redeemer's birth.

Yonder see His beacon shining,
  Angels to His glory sing :
God by these blest means designing
  To proclaim our Saviour King :
We would join the heavenly anthem,
And to Christ our tribute bring.

We would now, with heartfelt pleasure,
  As the wise men did of old,
Offer of our heart's best treasure,
  Which shall be as finest gold ;
Oh accept the humble offering,
Our heart's love for love untold.

There see Christ, the Lord of heaven,
  In a lowly manger laid :
His dear life for us was given,
  Who through sin from Him had strayed ;
Thus He left His bliss in heaven
For the creatures He had made.

Thy great gift is richer treasure,
　　More than gems or sparkling gold,
Yielding blessings without measure
　　With the hope of bliss untold ;
I would, loving Lord, most gracious
From Thy hands this treasure hold.

By R. J. FEARNLEY.

Text—"My Presence shall go with thee."

My gracious Saviour, Thou art here,
　　I would of Thy great wisdom learn,
I love to praise Thy name so dear,
　　My heart doth for Thy glory burn.

I pray that all along life's way
　　I may with Thee my Saviour go,
I want to hear Thee day by day
　　Tell me, my Lord, what shall I do.

Help me, dear Lord, to wait on Thee,
　　And love Thy blessed will to know,
And oh, reveal Thyself to me,
　　And tell me whither I shall go.

More of Thy grace to me be given,
　　That I may in Thine image grow,
And while I tread the way to heaven
　　May I Thy peace and favour know.

Through faith may I Thy glory see,
　　And ever conquer through Thy might,
Until I dwell at home with Thee,
　　And faith is ever lost in sight.

Still guide and keep me, O my God,
　　As through life's varied paths I go ;
Help me to bear the chastening rod,
　　And do Thy will while here below.

And when I tread the golden street,
   And wear the crown by Jesus given,
I'll praise and worship at Thy feet
   When I attain the bliss of Heaven.

By R. J. FEARNLEY.

Text—" At eventide there shall be light."

How favoured is that happy sage,
   Who, looking through life's varied way,
Sees God's design on every page,
   And knows His love hath ruled each day.

If he hath followed God's design,
   Whose wise unerring hand doth plan,
He now feels the sweet peace benign
   Of the God-fearing Christian man.

Who feels God's sweet and loving smile
   Doth on His child in old age rest,
Enjoys life's sunset, and the while
   Doth on his Saviour's bosom rest.

He feels as life draws to a close,
   As he thus lies on Jesu's breast,
How sweet for him thus to repose,
   In hope of an eternal rest.

God doth in His great love reveal
   Himself to every faithful saint,
And He will all His Word fulfil,
   To those who pray and never faint.

O loving Lord, my soul prepare
   For that unknown important day :
That I may through Thy mercy share
   Heaven's joys which never pass away.

And when the happy change shall come,
   My soul released from earth to be,
Oh may I reach my heavenly home
   Where I shall my dear Saviour see.

          By R. J. FEARNLEY.

Text—" The axe was borrowed."

IN our borrowed breath we feel it,
   We are weak and very frail ;
If it was not lent in mercy,
   Oh how soon our hearts would fail.

What a blessing from our Father
   Is the life He lends us here,
If we strive to do His pleasure,
   By His help sad hearts to cheer.

Oh how sweet kind words when given,
   In the spirit of His grace,
To the fainting and the weary,
   As we run the heavenly race.

Oft we feel His consolations
   In these hearts of flesh to rise,
Like the soft refreshing breezes
   Floating to us from the skies.

Soon these hearts will cease their beating,
   And our work will here be done,
Let us, then, keep toiling onward—
   Till we hear the welcome, Come.

Come, ye blessed of my Father,
   Drop these tools and cease your care ;
Now your working time is over,
   Yours are wages rich and rare ;

To be ever with our Saviour,
  In that heavenly land of rest,
Where God's saints are always happy,
  Praising Him among the blest.

By R. J. FEARNLEY.

*Text—" Blessed are the pure in heart, for they
        shall see God."*

WHEN shall my happy soul attain
  To heaven's unsullied joy,
Which God through His abounding grace
  Gives to his saints on high ?

I feel at times, while here below,
  Borne up on wings of love,
I do by faith obtain a glimpse
  Of heaven, my home above,

Where all who have obtained the prize
  Praise God in sweetest lays,
And now they with unveiléd eyes
  On their Redeemer gaze.

They fought with sternest foes while here,
  And often felt distressed,
And often gloomy doubt and fear
  Possessed their longing breast.

But now their cloudy days are o'er,
  Their struggles all have ceased,
And now they join with Christ their Lord
  In that eternal feast.

Faith now with them is lost in sight,
  They have the victory won,
Through Christ they dwell in endless light,
  And hear His glad well done.

Oh for a heart made free from sin,
    Loving and Christlike here,
Which will through faith in Jesus lead
    To bliss unsullied there.

By R. J. FEARNLEY.

Text—" *Where your treasure is, there will your heart*
          be also."

I HAD a precious treasure given
    Into my hands one day,
'Twas as a gem sent down from heaven
    To cheer life's coming day.

It was a casket sweet but frail,
    Wherein that jewel lay,
It would not bear rough handling, else
    'Twould break and pass away.

He was a bright and happy child,
    And was so dear to me,
I felt it made my heart so glad
    His loving face to see.

This precious treasure was to me
    A gift so rich and rare,
I felt not all the charms of earth
    Could with my boy compare.

I could not even bear to think
    I might be called to part
With one who could not fail to win
    A loving mother's heart.

But, ah ! the time came very soon
    That did my treasure take :
Before the sunny hour of noon
    That fragile casket brake.

And that sweet gem was borne away
    To deck the courts of heaven ;
There is a never-ending day
    Where spotless robes are given.

To all who have sought mercy here,
    And through our Saviour striven
To walk in paths of truth and grace,
    'Tis such who enter heaven.

Let all my best affections be
    Laid up on things above,
Where dear ones who have gone before
    Are waiting me in love.

And when I reach that happy place,
    And all heaven's treasures see,
I'll praise my Saviour who hath won
    This blessed home for me.

                  By R. J. FEARNLEY.

The above are a few lines which I wrote, having been requested to write a few for a mother who had a little boy which she loved very much taken away very suddenly by accident, which made her fret very much.

Text—"He hath borne our sins and carried our sorrows."

DEAR Lord, accept our humble praise,
For all Thy wondrous works and ways :
Thou hast Thy loving kindness shown
To us through all the way we've come.

Thou hast Thy richest love revealed,
To us Thy greatest promise sealed,
Thou hast a Prince and Saviour given
That we may taste the joys of heaven.

Oh what a gracious gift is this,
To pave our pathway right to bliss :
Our loving Lord the winepress trod
To bring our erring souls to God.

And Thou dost all our way prepare,
Thou dost our heaviest burdens bear,
It is Thy will that we should be
From every doubt and fear set free.

Help us, dear Saviour, still to hide,
Close in the hollow of Thy side,
Howe'er life's surging currents swell
I shall in peace and safety dwell.

Oh let me ever here below
Have Thy sweet presence where I go ;
And let Thy conquering grace be given,
So I shall dwell with Thee in heaven.

By R. J. FEARNLEY.

IMPROVE YOUR TALENTS.

WHAT a field for useful labour
    Is this world wherein we live,
And what time to use our talents
    Does our Heavenly Father give.

'Tis not that we should enfold them
    In a napkin white and clear,
But to use them for His glory
    Who has placed them in our care.

He has gone from us to heaven,
    There to stay a little while ;
He will soon be reappearing,
    With His sweet but solemn smile.

Where is the bright shining talent
    Which was freely given to thee ?
Hast not thou made some small efforts
    To convert it into three ?

There has been a golden harvest,
  Which thou shouldst have gathered in,
Thus becoming rich in blessing,
  Striving dying souls to win.

Making use of every talent,
  Comforting the sick and sad,
Thou shouldst thus have laid up treasure,
  Which wouldst make thine own heart glad.

O my loving Heavenly Father,
  Teach me to improve with care
Every talent Thou hast given me,
  So I may shine brighter there.

Thus, when I have run life's journey
  And the end of life is come,
I may hear Thee sweetly saying,
  To my happy soul, " Well done."

By R. J. FEARNLEY.

Text—" Build your house upon the Rock."

LET not the sandy shore delude your mind,
  As promising rich treasures from the deep,
Where the bright sunshine and the gentle wind
  Would woo the soul in fortitude to sleep.

For here are charming scenes of nature spread
  Before our unsuspecting longing eyes,
Here we shall from the richest valleys feed,
  And fruits of this world come as from the skies.

Pleasures abound, the skies are bright and clear,
  While fountains flow and water all around ;
Earth seems a garden, and its charms so dear,
  And palaces of pleasure stud the ground.

But all who dwell among this charming song
  Should have the richest jewel in their heart ;
They should to Christ, heaven's Priest and King, belong,
  From which not storms nor death can cause to part.

By R. J. FEARNLEY.

HOW TO COME TO JESUS.

LEAVE thy feelings, leave thy fears,
Leave thy labour, sighs, and tears,
Leave thy burden with thy Lord,
Take thy Saviour at His word ;
Let thy work of merit be
Trust in Him who died for thee.

By R. J. FEARNLEY.

Text—" God is light, and in Him is no darkness at all."

Thou, O my God, art pure,
  Dwelling in changeless light ;
Thy mercy ever shall endure,
  Mercy is Thy delight.

O make me free from sin,
  A semblance, Lord, of Thee ;
Spotless and clean, and pure within,
  I long, O God, to be.

Thou see'st all my path,
  My heart is known to Thee ;
O may I rest in Thee by faith,
  Till I Thy glory see.

I would not choose my way,
  But leave it in Thine hand ;
Thou ever art too wise to err,
  Too good to be unkind

Then let me still confide
   Each care and wish to Thee ;
O let me in Thy shelter hide,
   Reveal Thyself to me.

Still happy is my lot
   While Thou, my God, art near,
Let me be still and murmur not,
   Nor ever yield to fear.

Then let me, O my God,
   Be filled with Thy pure love,
O perfect me in every grace,
   And hide my life above.

My soul still thirsts for Thee,
   O fill me more and more ;
Still let me Thy great goodness see,
   And ever Thee adore.

                    By R. J. FEARNLEY.

Text—" I am weak but Thou art mighty."

O MAY we each, while here below,
Our heavenward course with joy pursue,
Looking to Him who will befriend
And keep us to our journey's end.

With Christ as guide, what shall we fear,
Though oft our path be thorny here,
O what if they but make us meet
To cast our crowns at Jesu's feet.

O may I still find shelter, Lord,
Reposing sweetly in Thy Word,
Which is a lamp unto my way,
And leads to everlasting day.

And though my sky be overcast,
O may Thy mercies in the past
Encourage me, that I may go
Still onward, leaving all below.

Then let me lean upon Thine arm,
Fearing no violence from the storm ;
O let me hide upon Thy breast,
And find in Thee a perfect rest.

Then O prepare me for that home,
That when my work on earth is done
I may be brought to heaven at last,
When all my warfare here is passed.

By R. J. Fearnley.

FROM PSALM XXIII.

The Lord my Shepherd is,
　　And often here I'd faint,
Were I not comforted by this,
　　I surely shall not want.

He makes me down to lie
　　In pastures fresh and green,
He leadeth me still waters by,
　　Where heavenly forms are seen.

My soul He doth restore
　　With drops of heavenly dew,
Thus helping me still more and more
　　My journey to pursue.

In paths of righteousness
　　Me He delights to take,
Still leading on to joy and peace,
　　E'en for His mercies' sake.

Still onward would I go,
  Though in God's Word it saith
I shall be called to travel through
  The mournful vale of death.

Nor would I yield to fear,
  Or ever be dismayed,
Since I have still my Shepherd here
  To brighten every shade.

Thy mercies are my staff,
  Thy promises my rod,
Help me to lean on these by faith,
  My Saviour and my God.

My table Thou dost spread
  In sight of all my foes,
With oil Thou dost anoint mine head,
  My cup with bliss o'erflows.

Thy mercy still shall flow
  To me through all my days,
Until I at Thy throne shall bow,
  And give Thee all the praise.

Then, when my work is done,
  And all my journey's past,
I'll ever dwell in peace at home
  With Thee, my God, at last.

                    By R. J. FEARNLEY.

ABSENCE OF GOD LAMENTED.

How tedious and tasteless the hours
  When Jesus no longer I see,
Sweet prospects, sweet birds, and sweet flowers,
  Have lost all their sweetness with me ;

C

The midsummer sun shines but dim,
   The fields strive in vain to look gay,
But when I am happy in Him
   December's as pleasant as May.

His Name yields the richest perfume,
   And sweeter than music His voice,
His presence disperses my gloom,
   And makes all within me rejoice ;
I should, were He always thus nigh,
   Have nothing to wish or to fear,
No mortal so happy as I,
   My summer would last all the year.

Content with beholding His face,
   My life to His pleasure resigned,
No changes of season or place
   Shall make any change in my mind.
While blest with a sense of His love,
   A palace a toy would appear ;
And prisons would palaces prove
   If Jesus would dwell with me there.

Dear Lord, if indeed I am thine,
   If Thou art my sun and my song,
Say why do I languish and pine,
   And why are my winters so long ?
O drive those dark clouds from the sky,
   Thy soul-cheering presence restore,
O take me unto Thee on high,
   Where winters and storms are no more.

               By R. J. FEARNLEY.

Text—" Give your heart to God now."

While in the calm bright morning
   Of springtide's earliest bloom,
My Saviour took my hand in His,
   And gently whispered, Come.

Heeding that gentle whisper,
  He placed His hand in mine,
And I then commenced life's journey,
  Led by His hand divine.

He urged me to press forward,
  Nor stay in sweetest bowers,
Where this world's charms seemed brightest,
  With music and with flowers.

He showed me that bright city,
  Most beauteous to behold,
Where the gates are decked with loveliest pearls,
  And streets with shining gold.

The longing He has given me
  To gain that happy home,
He has strengthened when I lingered,
  With his sweet accents, Come.

And, as I still press forward,
  I feel His strengthening hand
Helps my weak and faltering footsteps
  To press to that bright land.

I would not look behind me,
  Nor linger in the plains,
Since God has bid me come up higher,
  And trust for what remains.

So I would still go forward
  To that sweet home of bliss,
To be ever with my Saviour
  And bid adieu to this ;

Knowing not what we shall be
  In those sweet realms of day,
There are many glorious mansions
  I hear my Saviour say.

And as I journey onward,
  In sunny noontide's light,
May my faith be ever viewing
  That home so pure and bright.

By R. J. FEARNLEY.

THE PATH OF LIFE.

GOD hath a path marked out for me,
  In which my feet shall go,
And He will be my guard and guide
  And bring me safely through.

Thus on the path of life I'll press,
  By my dear Saviour given,
Which leads through paths of righteousness,
  And guides my soul to heaven.

And round me spread on every hand
  Are plains of living green;
Yonder is a sweet shady bower,
  There flows the living stream.

And here I may awhile partake
  Of waters pure and sweet,
Which shall refresh my thirsty soul,
  And bathe my weary feet.

Thus whilst I in the shade repose,
  Under His sheltering wing,
Here I can sweetly meditate,
  And of His mercies sing.

But I must up and travel on
  Before the day is gone,
Knowing that every passing hour
  Still brings me nearer home.

And now I must the mount ascend
  Which taxes all my strength,
And I am cheered by God's sweet Word,
  I shall o'ercome at length.

Fear not, for I have overcome
  Life's ills and cares for thee,
And holding firmly to My hand,
  I will thine helper be.

Thus I must climb the rugged mount
  If I its heights attain,
And though it is a toilsome path
  It shall be for my gain.

And now I've reached the mountain top
  God bids me look around,
And truly while I look I feel
  This place is hallowed ground.

And while I look on rapturous scenes
  Which God to me hath given,
I see beyond the clear blue sky
  The pearly gates of heaven.

And whilst I thus enraptured gaze
  Upon those realms of light,
The blessed thought comes to my heart
  There is no sin nor night.

Now that Thou hast to me vouchsafed
  Such precious views of heaven,
O let Thy presence go with me
  And conquering grace be given.

Thus when I reach my journey's end,
  Led by Thy loving hand,
I shall be borne on wings of love
  To heaven, that better land.

          By R. J. FEARNLEY.

THE JOY SET BEFORE US.

Thou dost fit up our mansions there,
Thou dost for us a place prepare,
And all who listen to Thy voice
Shall trusting in Thy word rejoice.

And when we reach that happy shore,
Where sin and death shall be no more,
We'll join with the triumphant throng
To sing the everlasting song.

Amid those streets of shining gold
I shall not feel I'm growing old ;
I oft feel weak and languid here
But there I shall not shed one tear.

Praise God for all His mercies given,
But I shall praise Him more in heaven,
There I shall sing in noblest lays
The wonders of redeeming grace.

There in those palaces so bright,
There shall be neither sin nor night,
There shall no sorrow there be seen
On those sweet shores for ever green.

God will to us in heaven restore
Glory and joy for evermore,
There we shall from our labour rest,
And dwell with Him among the blest.

By R. J. FEARNLEY.

PRAISE FOR GOD'S REDEEMING LOVE.

I'LL praise my God who died for me,
He paid my debt on calvary ;
He bore the cross, endured the shame,
To suffer in my place He came.

Leaving His beauteous home on high,
Quitting His throne beyond the sky,
He came in meek humility
To be despised and die for me.

To raise my fainting faltering heart,
In all my griefs He bears a part ;
He knows my sorrows, hears my prayers,
He hears my sighs and counts my tears.

To comfort mourning hearts He came,
Glory and praise to His dear Name ;
He loves to give the weary rest,
And all who come to Him are blest.

I hear His sweet and loving voice,
Bidding my troubled heart rejoice
In Him who bore my sin and shame,
And in my stead to die He came.

He gives His strength and grace to all
Who for His grace and mercy call ;
The lost He suffered to redeem,
He saves each soul who comes to Him.

By R. J. FEARNLEY.

HIS GRACE IS SUFFICIENT FOR ME.

In my dear Redeemer
  There is joy and rest,
I have found a pillow
  On His loving breast ;
In His arms of mercy
  I have found repose ;
Jesus gives me comfort,
  He my sorrow knows.

He has spoken to me
　When my heart was sad :
" I am thy salvation,
　I will make thee glad ;
I have suffered for thee
　On the rugged tree,
I have paid thy ransom,
　I have set thee free."

In His tender mercy
　He has me forgiven,
He has paved my pathway
　Right from earth to heaven ;
In His every promise
　I am truly blest,
In His great redemption
　I have found sweet rest.

In His own rich garments
　He my soul hath clad,
Through His grace and mercy
　He hath made me glad.
I would still press forward,
　In my Saviour's might,
Till I see His glory,
　With His saints in light.

There in songs of rapture,
　And in noblest lays,
I would join the ransomed
　His dear name to praise.
He has passed before me
　To those realms of light,
I would dwell for ever
　In His loving sight.

By R. J. FEARNLEY.

WHILST THINKING ON GOD'S GOODNESS.

In the hours when sin and sorrow
  Would have torn my aching breast,
I have found a perfect refuge
  And a place wherein to rest.

When the little bark is tossing
  On the ocean's troubled wave,
Wondering where to find a harbour
  Or a hand that's quick to save,

Suddenly, when thickest darkness
  Has o'erspread the sky above,
There has been a gracious Saviour
  Full of sympathy and love.

Walking on the troubled waters,
  He has come to my relief,
He has seen my time of peril,
  And has felt my bitter grief.

He has bid me cast my anchor,
  And has caused my bark to land
In a place of rest and beauty,
  Reaching out His loving hand.

He has brought me through sweet meadows,
  Where the living fountains flow,
Causing me to reap rich blessing
  While I tread these vales below.

So my gentle, loving Saviour
  Leads me on to joys on high,
Where he has fit up my mansion
  In His home beyond the sky.

                              By R. J. FEARNLEY.

Text —" Fear thou not, for I am with thee."

As I tread my pilgrim pathway
  Jesus keeps my soul in love,
He is watching all my journey
  From His glorious home above.

He who trod life's chequered pathway,
  Bearing all my sin and shame,
He it is whom I will honour,
  Giving glory to His name.

When my steps grow faint and falter,
  In the rugged way I take,
He has come and gently led me,
  For His love and mercy's sake.

So I would keep pressing onward,
  Since He doth my way prepare,
I can trust His love and mercy,
  He doth all my sorrows share.

When my journey here is ended,
  And my pilgrimage is o'er,
I shall be with Thee, my Saviour,
  I shall praise Thee evermore.

                    By R. J. FEARNLEY.

Text—" Thy loving-kindness is better than life."

OH ! what is all the world to me
Until I here Thy beauty see,
Until I realise Thy love,
And feel Thy drawings from above.

Until I feel Thy kindly hand
Is leading to a brighter land,
Then all along my path shall shine
A heavenly radiancy divine.

I then shall know Thy favour sure,
Nor doubt Thy loving kindness more ;
So long as trusting in Thy Word
I cleave with purpose to my Lord.

Thy love is ever still the same,
For love is Thy distinguished name :
I here would at Thy footstool fall,
And own Thee gracious Lord of all.

Be this the purpose of my heart,
Ever to choose the better part,
Then I shall own when life shall end,
Thou art my never failing friend.

By R. J. FEARNLEY.

Text—"All Thy works praise Thee."

WHEN we look far above us,
   In yon clear heaven of light,
Across those clear blue portals
   Roll silvery clouds so bright.

The sun in all his splendour
   Shines forth with radiant beams,
Reflecting his bright image
   Upon clear flowing streams.

There in the pleasant meadow,
   All carpeted with green,
And decked with sweetest flowers,
   The peaceful herds are seen.

The little song-bird warbling
   In sweetest notes doth fly,
With its light wings extended,
   It mounts far up on high.

Thus, everything around us
  Bids us to look above,
With praise and adoration
  To that great God of love.

Who hath in love and mercy
  Given life and peace to me,
And says 'tis but a shadow
  Of that which is to be.

The fountain and the forest,
  The moorland and the dell,
All join to swell the chorus,
  Our Father's praise to tell.

But Oh ! dear Lord and Saviour,
  We never can proclaim
In words and tones the sweetest
  The virtues of Thy name.

By R. J. FEARNLEY.

Text —" The peace of God, which passeth knowledge."

As we tread life's pleasant pathway,
  Walking through the meadows sweet,
We are charmed with nature's blossoms,
  Which are scattered at our feet.

In the cool refreshing streamlet,
  With its waters calm and bright,
We can see the sun depicted,
  Sending forth its glorious light.

When we look upon the waters
  Rolling on with silent ease,
How the scene around reminds us
  Of the soul who feels at peace.

He who feels in rich possession
   Of the hope through Jesus given,
Feels through faith the happy prospect
   Of the perfect rest in heaven.

Where our hearts shall swell with rapture,
   While our eyes for ever gaze,
Steadfastly and never tiring,
   On our dear Redeemer's face.

There we'll rest with Christ for ever,
   In that land of pure delight ;
When we've crossed the silent river,
   Then our faith is lost in sight.

Thou wilt keep Thy children faithful,
   If we look to Thee alone ;
And when all our work is finished,
   We shall hear Thee say, Well done.

By R. J. FEARNLEY.

Text —"*For I the Lord thy God will hold thy right hand, saying unto thee, Fear not, for I will help thee.*"

LORD, help me humbly in Thy sight to stand,
     Nor yield to fear ;
Since Thou art holding to me Thy right hand,
     Thy word so dear
Assures me that my path, as marked by Thee,
Shall prove the best, and for my profit be.

I would not ask that Thou would always take
     'Neath sunny skies,
But that Thou wilt e'en for Thy mercies' sake
     Make me all-wise,
So that I may o'ercome the powers of sin,
And in Thy name life's every battle win.

And though at times life's way be dark and drear,
  I in Thy strength
Shall meet the foe, nor yield to doubt or fear,
  Until at length
Brought through the darkness by the wings of faith,
I shall, through Thee, o'ercome the powers of death.

And when Thou hast, through Thy almighty power,
  Saved me, the least,
Through chequered paths, and at life's latest hour
  To heaven's glad feast,
I would adore, and give Thee all the praise
For Thy great love, through never-ending days.

By R. J. FEARNLEY.

PART II.

HERE are a few poor feeble words
  Offered for Jesu's sake;
Oh may our all-wise loving Lord
  Each one a blessing make.

And may a silent messenger
  Bind up some broken heart,
Oh may some soul in heaven appear
  Who did again take heart.

By H. A. FEARNLEY.

TIME IS SHORT.

SWIFTLY do the moments fly,
Bearing record up on high,
Some of battles fought and won,
And of bravest actions done;
Some of cowardly despair—
Ah, instead of faith and prayer—
And of words and deeds unblest,
Stealing bliss from many a breast.

Time is ever on the wing,
With the past e'er mingling,
And it is for us to prize
It above all earthly toys;
May we make each moment bright,
Ever noble to the sight,
That e'en angels' holy gaze
Will approve our works and ways.

Let us, by some word we speak,
Heal the hearts that well-nigh break,
As the gentle falling dew
Doth the withering flowers renew;
Oh may we each moment fill,
That it will at last reveal
A sweet picture to the view
At the last great, grand review.

May we lead some souls that droop
To behold the star of hope;
Bring some weary wanderer back
To the glad and heavenward track;
Knowing that each moment gone
Is a priceless jewel flown,
Which our Saviour sends us down
Yet to glisten in a crown.

By H. A. FEARNLEY.

Text—"*All Thy works praise Thee.*"

O HEAVENLY Father earth is bright,
   Its flowers are beauteous, gay,
And birds are singing with delight,
   Throughout the livelong day.

The glad creation called by Thee,
   In skill and power divine,
To life and glorious liberty,
   In Thy great bounty shine.

The day reveals in glowing light
  Nature's most lovely scenes,
Turning the soul and wondering sight
  To holier, higher themes.

When the dark mantle of the night
  Veils the fair grandeur seen,
We gaze on the celestial orbs—
  The moon and stars' bright beams.

But oh, when we remember Thee,
  Who made and cares for all,
Thy love is a great mystery,
  Which thrills the enraptured soul.

For man, whom Thou didst make so pure,
  In Thine own image shone,
Did not the testing time endure,
  But e'en defied Thy throne.

Our hearts would praise the boundless love
  Which sin yet more revealed,
Which evermore doth faithful prove,
  And hath the sinner healed.

While holy angels veil their face,
  Oh, it is bliss to know,
That we may on Thy beauty gaze,
  And bear the radiant glow.

By H. A. FEARNLEY.

Text—" He doeth all things well."

HELP us to learn to praise Thee, Lord,
When life its brilliant joys afford ;
When pain doth rack the throbbing breast,
In hope's glad rays may I find rest.

Oh, may we praise for every good,
'Mid sorest trial trust our God ;
Nor e'er Thy loving-kindness grieve,
By our poor erring unbelief.

May we still realise that pain
Can work for us eternal gain,
When trustfully and bravely passed,
Our joys will e'en the sweeter taste.

After the piercing crown of thorn,
Bright gems the victors' brows adorn ;
And every soul that conquers here
Shall praise Thee for the grief and tear.

Then let us every cross take up,
E'er drink the mixture in our cup ;
Knowing God's hand is tenderness,
And that whate'er He gives will bless.

And when our reason's eye is dim,
May faith more firmly cling to Him,
Who will in heaven's clear light reveal
The love that ruled His sovereign will.

Help us, O Lord, at Thy blest feet,
To sit and learn till counted meet
For Thy loved voice to call us higher,
Refined as gold by purging fire.

By H. A. FEARNLEY.

Text—" Thy loving-kindness is better than life."

How precious is Thy holy smile,
  My Saviour and my God ;
It nerves the weary heart for toil,
  Though rugged be the road.

When ready to give up the task,
　And tempted to despair,
Thy gentle voice doth bid me ask,
　I all thy griefs did bear.

Yea, God hath given all my good,
　And waiteth to bestow
Bright sunshine, clothing, daily food,
　All beauteous nature's show.

For He who sees the sparrow's fall,
　And clothes the lilies fair,
Will give His needy children all,
　E'en bliss beyond compare.

And when His face shall be revealed,
　Thou then shalt understand,
That mercy wounded but to heal,
　And love the whole hath planned.

Oh help us, Lord, to join our praise,
　With the white-robed above ;
Daily our grateful hearts to raise,
　Tuned by triumphant love.

By H. A. FEARNLEY.

Text—" My presence shall go with thee."

GOD of our life, again morn's orient light
Has burst in beauty on our waking sight ;
Our reasoning powers have been by Thee restored,
Oh be Thy name by all Thy saints adored.

May my first love and warmest thoughts be Thine,
Kindled by guardian care and love divine ;
On the glad wings of faith, may prayer arise,
With my first breath, a fragrant sacrifice.

Ah, may I tread each day in footmarks bright
In my dear Saviour's, e'en from morn till night;
And may each footprint left by me behind
Lead some lost soul the golden street to find.

When pressing on 'neath noontide's burning sun,
May I not faint until the task is done,
Nor tire, while following Thee to pastures green,
To richer fruits than e'er by Eden seen.

Thus, gaining strength, I'll press to scenes more fair
Than lips on earth can portray or compare,
To yonder city with its jasper walls,
Its mansions, where no shadow ever falls.

When life's sure sunset gilds the glorious west,
Arrayed in gorgeous colours, tells of rest
To all the weary, may I then appear
In heaven's white robe, and Jesu's image bear.

Oh may I hear sweet notes from angel's lyre,
And hear my Jesus calling me up higher,
And catch a glimpse of heaven's pearly gate,
While for my coming Lord I longing wait.

By H. A. FEARNLEY.

GOD CHANGETH NOT.

AND now another year has flown,
　　And on the wings of love were borne,
Mercy with night, and every dawn,
　　Though some sad hearts are sorely torn.

From many are their loved ones fled,
　　To triumph in immortal life;
We will not say that they are dead,
　　But are set free from care and strife.

Oh, how the starlit heavens have shone
    Upon us all, to cheer the lone ;
The brilliant days and sunny noon
    Often have charmed us every one.

Its mercies have been far more vast
    Than mortal mind can e'er recount,
Wider than thought, beyond request,
    They e'en to highest heaven do mount.

Swifter than dove's light wing can dart,
    Christ's love has to salvation flown ;
And thrilled the weary, drooping heart,
    Dispersing all its dread and gloom.

Oh may love's mighty wings still bear
    My soul above all doubt and sin,
Until set free from every snare
    Thou bring'st eternal victory in.

                By H. A. FEARNLEY.

Text—" O rest in the Lord."

As silent falls the evening shade,
    My soul, renew the wondrous theme
Of God's vast love which ne'er doth fade,
    But more 'tis viewed the brighter beams.

And now whilst nature, hushed to rest,
    Doth 'neath Thy tender eye repose,
Oh may I lean on Jesu's breast,
    And heaven's sweet peace mine eyelids close.

While moon and star e'er brightly shine,
    Sweet tokens of Thy matchless power ;
Oh may Thy precious form divine
    Still guard Thy children every hour.

May holy seraphim surround
   Thy loved ones' couch, and all their homes,
Heaven's music sweet all sorrows drown,
   And make us feel we're nearer home.

May heavenly visions cheer the hearts
   Of sick and weary, sad and lone ;
And the true light which ne'er departs,
   Dispel all fear, disperse all gloom.

When life's last eventide we see,
   Its rich-hued colours in the west,
May Christ unlock heaven's gate for me,
   And crown another victor blest.

Then shall the courts and mansions fair
   Ring with sweet praises to our King,
Faith end in bliss beyond compare,
   And we our hallelujahs sing.

By H. A. FEARNLEY.

Text—" Lo I am with thee alway."

LORD, let me walk with Thee,
   Though weakness be my lot ;
In patience, hope, and charity,
   E'er trust and murmur not.

And may I willing learn
   The lessons taught to me,
Until all evil I shall spurn
   And live in purity.

Oh lead me, Saviour, dear,
   Through good or seeming ill,
Until I Thy bright image bear,
   And only choose Thy will

Through weakness then shall glow
　Thy perfect grace divine,
Thy strength alone can make me grow,
　And for my Saviour shine.

By H. A. FEARNLEY.

THOU KNOWEST, LORD.

THOU know'st my way, O Lord my God,
　When I bewildered stand :
Oh give me strength to bear the load,
Oh gently use Thy chastening rod,
　And firmly grasp my hand.

Let every link in life's strange chain,
　Mysterious though it be,
Though skill divine permit my pain,
Work heaven's design, eternal gain,
　Till I its beauty see.

If I would in Thy footsteps tread,
　I must like Thee know grief,
If there should come what most I dread,
I only suffer like mine Head,
　And Thou dost bring relief.

So I shall conquer through the cross,
　E'en dark Gethsemane,
And loose but sin, that cruel dross,
As gold refined, rise through its loss,
　And heavenly lustre gain.

Since glory ends what grace begun,
　And Thou art e'er my guide,
At rosy morn or sultry noon,
May I still say "Thy will be done,"
　Since Thou with me abide.

And when the eventide's glad light
   Reveals the pearly gate,
To my winged thought and raptured sight,
May Heaven's beams burst through it bright,
   And Jesus for me wait.

By H. A. FEARNLEY.

THE DAY OF REST.

ANOTHER glorious Sabbath morn
   Hath breathed on us its golden dawn,
Oh help us, Lord, with heart sincere,
   Its boundless mercies now to own.

Its rosy light upon my way
   Awakes again faith's wondering sight,
To gaze upon Heaven's cloudless day,
   Where is no sin or gloomy night.

Oh may it wake within my heart
   True gratitude and burning love,
And may I in God's praise take part,
   And vie with angel choirs above.

While nature in rich beauty glows,
   And all creation speaks of Thee,
May I take up the language too,
   And all through life reflect but Thee.

Like birds amid rich blooming bowers,
   May I Thy sweetest anthems raise ;
Like fairest fruits and fragrant flowers,
   May I lend charm to all my days.

May all the glorious landscapes here
   Lead me to adore my God the more ;
May beauty guide, nor e'er ensnare,
   But lead me to heaven's fadeless shore.

By H. A. FEARNLEY.

Text—"*Blessed is the man that trusteth in Him.*"

How blessed is the child of God,
    Whose refuge is beneath His wing,
Through sunshine bright, on thorny road,
    His soul secure, God's praise can sing.

Yea, God doth lead in pleasant ways,
    Rejoicing he doth follow on ;
When the cloud hides the sun's bright rays
    His love doth whisper, clouds are gone.

If he must wear a crown of thorn
    And climb the mount where Christ hath trod,
He shall behold a glorious dawn
    And hold communion with his God.

Our Lord's almighty love and power
    Shall turn all seeming ill to good,
And lead to the triumphant hour
    Even through fire or swelling flood.

Thus shall he journey safely on,
    Nor fairest scenes his soul allure ;
Steadfast in faith whate'er may come,
    Life's weal or woe, he shall endure.

O Thou who art all-wise and good,
    Give to my heart all-conquering grace ;
Thy will be done, nor be withstood
    Whilst I am locked in thine embrace.

While faith beholds Thy smiling face,
    Though here I may not understand
Thy guidance or its meaning trace,
    I'll know it in the better land.

By H. A. FEARNLEY.

Text—" The love of God passeth knowledge."

THE love of Jesus is to me a deep unfathomed mystery;
To think He did earth's desert tread, and not a place to lay
    His head;
To think though God, by hosts adored and Lord of the
    creation, He
Should leave His royal throne above, to be a sacrifice for
    me.
See how the multitude He feeds, nor cares for his own
    pressing needs;
Though Heaven's King, He doth bestow all good to heal
    His creatures woe.
He even came in human form, to face and brave the
    keenest storm,
Nay, more, to suffer for our sin, to bring us endless victory
    in.
So hath our God, in human form, our sorest griefs and
    sorrows borne;
Himself an offering for our sin, to bring us Heaven's glad
    rising beam.
Behold Him, bearing heavier load than e'er was borne
    except by God,
Climbing the Mount of Olivet, bearing dread agony and
    sweat;
See Him in yonder garden now, while holy angels soothe
    His brow,
To comfort Him, if possible, while conquering the hosts of
    hell.
Yet e'en His loved disciples sleep, while love with Him
    should pray and weep;
But Jesus says, "Thy will be done," and goes to meet the
    sinner's doom.
Ah! yet he bore the thorny crown, the wicked scoff, and
    awful frown,
And one did e'en his Lord deny in sight of men, of hell,
    and sky.
The Lord of glory calmly goes to Calvary, led by His
    foes;

And love doth fill his throbbing heart, while pity fain would
    take their part :
His power could strike the mocker down, but love would
    give them each a crown ;
Like to the wretched, dying thief, He fain would fly to their
    relief ;
Yet they will nail Him to the cross, accounting holiness as
    dross.
Cruel, His writhing nerves did tear, but love and meekness
    all doth bear ;
"Father," He cries, "forgive them now, for oh, they know
    not what they do ; "
And then 'neath sun-forsaken sky, yea, "It is finished,"
    floats on high.
And now, methinks, by faith I see angels bear palms of
    victory ;
Myriads of shining harps of gold, playing the glad new
    song now told,
Proclaiming pardon from our God, who now hath sheathed
    Justice's dread sword.
Oh may we all unite to praise the wonders of redeeming
    grace,
Until in Heaven its fulness beams, in holy rapture, living
    streams.

By H. A. FEARNLEY.

Text—" Trust in God, and fear not."

WE'LL praise Thee, Lord, when skies are blue,
    And sun is shining bright,
And for the gently falling dew,
    Sparkling with rainbow light.

We praise Thee for the ocean wave,
    Beauteous with silvery spray,
Whose waters every shore do lave,
    In regions far away.

We praise Thee for the gentle showers,
  Though skies be darkened o'er,
Refreshing, fragrant, drooping flowers,
  Displaying Thy great power.

The cloud may hide the sunny rays
  Whose brightness cheers the soul :
Mercy awhile forbids our gaze,
  That nature be made whole.

The ocean, in its grandeur wild,
  May rage in dashing foam,
Thrilling Thy still, admiring child,
  Lest some may find sad doom.

We'll praise Thee, Lord, for all glad sights,
  And 'mid life's mystery,
When love doth hide its glorious face,
  May faith e'er cling to Thee.

Then we can praise Thee here awhile,
  Though all around be veiled :
We can rejoice while Thy blest smile
  O'er gloom and haze prevail.

By H. A. FEARNLEY.

GOD IS LIFE AND LOVE.

Thou God of nature and of grace,
  As on Thy wondrous works I gaze,
My soul is thrilled with pure delight,
  But cannot comprehend Thy might.

While skill most beauteous I see,
  I cannot sound love's mystery,
Which brings to us such forms of grace,
  Such charming scenes in every place.

The rolling seas obey Thy will,
　　Obeying yet Thy " Peace, be still " ;
Whether its waves dash mountains high,
　　Or calm reflect the clear blue sky.

The woodland shade with blossomed spray
　　And lovely songsters charms our way,
And bids us 'neath its shelter rest,
　　And join to swell the chorus blest.

The valley, clothed in verdant green,
　　Its sparkling fount and silvery stream,
Its orchards rich with fruit and flowers,
　　Remind us of fair Eden's bowers.

But when the rugged mount I climb,
　　The view I gain is most sublime ;
Methinks that words all fail to tell
　　Of God's vast love unsearchable.

But, oh ! what joy to realise
　　The bliss that waits us in the skies,
When man shall in God's image shine,
　　And in eternal light divine.

The vast and beautiful will then
　　Be crowned with heaven's diadem ;
All glory then to God be given,
　　Who maketh bright both earth and heaven.

All mystery then shall be revealed,
　　All revelation be unsealed ;
And e'er in Jesu's face we'll see
　　The spring of all felicity.

　　　　　　　　　　By H. A. FEARNLEY.

Text—"Faith is the gift of God."

PRAYER is the cry of anguish deep,
    'Mid sorrow and distress ;
But faith doth know, though eyes may weep,
    That God will surely bless.

Prayer is the swift-winged message flown
    Into our Father's ear ;
Faith nestles 'neath His sheltering throne
    And patient waiteth there.

Prayer bursteth from the breaking heart
    In bitter sighs and groans ;
Faith bids the awful gloom depart
    And e'er God's mercy owns.

Prayer cryeth 'neath the thunder-cloud
    When light is fled away :
Faith sees behind a smiling God
    Who lightning's power doth sway.

Prayer is the voice of agony
    In yonder garden lone,
While faith doth God in all things see,
    And says, "Thy will be done."

Prayer asketh now for all things good,
    That it may see no frown,
But faith beholds beyond the flood
    A beauteous glittering crown.

A crown by the dear Saviour given,
    Bought by His precious blood ;
A mansion in yon glorious heaven,
    Prepared, adorned by God.

Prayer moves the mighty power on high,
    While faith God's hand doth grasp;
The wondrous love of Deity
    Gives more than tongue doth ask.

Yea, through the atoning sacrifice
    The prayer of faith He hears,
And showers rich bounties from the skies,
    E'en joys beyond compare.

Prayer at morn, noon, and eventide
    Should breathe thanksgiving sweet;
By faith upheld, accompanied,
    As fragrant incense meet.

By H. A. FEARNLEY.

Text—" Let your light shine."

OH ! what a glorious mission methinks the sun has given,
One of the brightest, gladdest of nature under heaven ;
We should not see rare colours on rainbow-glistening dew,
Nor richest tints of flowers God's skill hath given too ;
The dashing waves of ocean would yield no silvery spray,
'Twould lose its charms of beauty were sunshine called away.
What myriads of flowers it calls to a new birth,
Wayside and fragrant bowers in bounty bring them forth ;
It steals in humble cottage on its glad mission free,
With grand, though silent, message to poorest souls that be ;
It brings to many a sad one, pictures of lovely scenes
Beyond its height and lustre where glow life's endless beams.
Oh how my heart would falter to see it e'er go down,
Were it not hope that whispered again of its return.
O Father, may I praise Thee for sun and all things fair,
And more may I e'er love Thee for joys that all may share.
Thus may I vie with nature and only live to shine,
Only reflecting Jesus, in His true light divine ;
Where'er I go may brightness a halo cast around
My daily life and footsteps, Thy grace in me abound ;

And may I lead some wanderer to heights of bliss untold,
And bring some lost, though loved one, into the shepherd's
　　fold.
Thus I may shed a lustre which some poor soul may see,
And lead the sad and lowly by sweetest charity,
Where joys can never wither, nor beauty fade away,
Where all in Christ's own likeness praise Him through
　　endless day.

By H. A. FEARNLEY.

Text—"*For I the Lord thy God will hold thy right hand,
　　saying, 'Fear not, for I will help thee.'*"
—ISAIAH, Chap. xli.

WHILST Thou dost hold mine hand,
　　I need not fear;
The way I may not understand,
　　But Thou art here.

Though dangers threaten me,
　　And thunder cloud
May hide Thy smile away,
　　Yet Thou art God.

When flowers deck the way
　　I may not grasp,
All, all is well, whilst Thou
　　Mine hand doth clasp.

Some of life's fairest flowers
　　Most poisonous are,
Whose graces deck rich bowers,
　　But life might mar.

Were brightest charms of earth
　　All given to me,
Their noblest, highest worth
　　I might not see.

Should they allure my soul
　　To leave Thy side,
All joys would flee away
　　Without my guide.

O Father, lead me on,
　　With me abide ;
Then grief and cares are flown
　　And wicked pride.

For while with Thee I walk
　　All brighter grows ;
Thy sweetest voice doth bring
　　Humble repose.

So we together climb
　　To higher bliss ;
To heavenly spheres sublime,
　　Through love and peace.

　　　　　　By H. A. FEARNLEY.

Text—" Behold the Lilies, how they grow."

METHINKS I see a lovely flower
　　Blooming in richness in yon field ;
Though gracing not a rosy bower,
　　Humbly its fragrance it doth yield.

It may be that some passer by
　　Will halt to admire its petals fair,
Or that the traveller carelessly
　　Heeds not its glowing charms so rare.

But hark, one day my Saviour draws
　　A glorious picture from its bloom ;
I think I see Him kindly pause
　　To bring to all a lesson home.

To those who listen to His words,
  And anxious are to catch their strains,
This flower a vision grand affords
  Of God's great care and bounteous reign.

Yea, even Solomon, He says,
  Was not arrayed like one of these,
In all the splendour of his days,
  For God their beautifier is.

Lord, grant my soul may now be dressed
  In Thy rich robes of righteousness,
For while adorned with such a dress
  E'en angels will admire its grace.

Thus may I through Thy beauty lead
  Some soul to Thee who clothes and feeds
The hungry, thirsty multitude,
  And without price supplies their needs.

May meekness and humility
  E'er crown my head whate'er my lot ;
May I grow daily more like Thee,
  Reflecting what Thy love hath wrought.

Thus may I live to glorify
  Thee, whose great skill all beauty forms,
Till Heaven's matchless purity,
  Redeeming grace, my soul adorns.

By H. A. FEARNLEY.

Text—" Hope is the anchor of the soul."

While viewing lovely scenes one day
  My soul was filled with glad delight,
But thinking they must fade away
  My joy would soon have taken flight,

Had not a gentle whisper sweet
    Soothed all the sorrow threatening me,
Saying that far more glorious scenes
    I should again with rapture see.

Ah, 'twas a charming heavenly voice
    Which darted swift to comfort me,
It made my throbbing heart rejoice
    And stilled all my perplexity.
And e'er in time of dread or fear
    It's whisper sweet was "Calmly wait,"
I felt as though some angel near
    Had sped right from the mercy-seat.

Ah, yes, it gilt with shining ray
    The edge of each o'erhanging cloud ;
'Twas hope that spoke of cloudless day
    When tempest voice was raging loud.
'Tis blessed hope, but known through faith,
    Which guards the dangerous, rugged way ;
Comes quick to save poor souls from death,
    And turneth darkness into day.

'Tis faith endures the awful storm,
    And nerves the soul to bear all pain,
Till hope's most timely, glittering form
    Helps it to climb to endless gain.
Hope casts a gleam across the wave,
    And shows a far more wealthy land,
Where all who will each peril brave
    Shall yet receive a portion grand.

Hope points to yonder rainbow light,
    When clouds their lavish waters pour,
Showing its radiant colours bright,
    The witness of God's love and power.
Without this gracious light of heaven
    All efforts droop, all gloom prevails,
No heed to nobler life is given,
    All charm to glorious actions fails.

The vessel tossing helplessly,
  Without an anchor drifts along,
Strikes the sharp rocks amid deep sea,
  And sinks, and is forever gone.
While God is mine, blest hope my star,
  In Jesu's great redemption I
Shall triumph, though its lustre far
  At times doth gleam to my weak eye.

Thank God for faith which knows His hand
  Is holding mine, and guides to bliss,
For hope in a strange pilgrim land,
  Which grasps it, feels its warmth and peace.
I need not dread while led by hope,
  That hope which Jesus left behind ;
Whate'er my lot 'twill bear me up,
  I e'er shall heaven's rich blessings find.

While I advance toward my home,
  More glorious will its prospects be,
Until within full sight I come,
  And its fair jasper walls I see ;
Until the welcome I shall hear,
  And safe pass through the pearly gate,
And God shall dry the last sad tear,
  And glory charms my wondering sight.

                    By H. A. FEARNLEY.

Text—" The greatest of these is Charity."

  SWEET Charity, methinks I see
    Thy noble visage crowned
  With richer gems than e'er can be
    In worldly treasures found ;
  Thy heart is full of tenderness,
    And pity for mankind ;
  Thou dost at all times love and bless,
    With soul, with heart and mind.

Patiently bearing every ill,
　　All rude malign and scorn,
Nothing but love thou dost reveal,
　　Doth naught but good return.
Believing the sad tale of grief,
　　Thy sympathy doth flow,
Doth gladly aid, and for relief,
　　E'en would thyself bestow.

Is never proud, when bravest deeds
　　Have won thee high renown,
But seeth more the soul's great needs
　　Than its own jewelled crown.
Ah ! Charity is sweeter far
　　Than the most fragrant bowers,
More brilliant than yon glittering star,
　　Most rich in all its dowers.

Its fruits are sweeter to the taste,
　　The more of them we know,
Ripe with the flow of heavenly grace,
　　Rich flavour doth bestow.
A branch of the fair tree of life,
　　Its fruit is love divine,
Through mystery, mid woe and strife,
　　It doth the brighter shine.

Charity seeketh not its own,
　　But God's great glory here,
To raise poor souls, by sin trod down,
　　Unto a higher sphere.
It glorieth in God's great love,
　　And strives to make it known,
To lead the lost to courts above,
　　Fair gems for Jesu's crown.

　　　　　　　　　By H. A. FEARNLEY.

GOD IS THE FATHER OF LIGHTS.

FATHER of lights, in whose replendent rays
　We see great wonders wrought in life's strange ways ;
Beauties which Thou alone can'st e'er reveal,
　Which love and grace alone to us unveil.

Oh, help us, Lord, to covet but Thy smile
　On all our way 'mid weariness or toil ;
Then led by Thee we cannot go astray,
　While Thou disperse dark gloom which all doth spoil.

Sorrow to gladness Thou shalt ever turn,
　Thy comfort soothe the saddest hearts that weep ;
While the rich lessons of Thy grace we learn,
　While our frail barks are tossed upon the deep.

We'll tread with Thee the rugged mountain steep,
　Nor shrink while Thou dost firmly grasp our hand,
For strength almighty our frail steps doth keep,
　The summit gained we'll view the better land.

Thy glorious smile doth cast a halo round,
　Which lights our path and leads us safe and blest,
'Mid thorn and brier on to holy ground,
　Where all is heavenly beauty, joy, and rest.

Thus shall all darkness yield to glorious day,
　The bitter end in blooming fragrance sweet ;
And when we reach the end of life's strange way,
　Untiring we will e'er Thy love repeat.

By H. A. FEARNLEY.

DARKNESS SHALL TURN TO DAY.

(A birthday wish to my dear sister.)

GOD bless thy birthday is my prayer,
May He be with thee everywhere ;
And oh, may each succeeding year
Brighter with heavenly light appear.

Oh may thy path more charming glow
With heavens smile dispelling woe,
And may thy God feel e'er more near,
Thy head to raise, Thy heart to cheer.

In heavenly radiance may Thy soul
Be dressed, in Jesu's love made whole,
Till He to thy glad eyes appear,
The fairest rose, the morning star.

By H. A. FEARNLEY.

*Text—" He is the chief among ten thousand, and altogether
lovely."*

O HEAVENLY Father, precious Saviour, now
    Accept our heaven-born praise at morn,
For sweet repose and tender care bestowed,
    For strength renewed and reason's bright return.

Accept our praise for every power lent,
    And may our first and highest thoughts be Thine;
May every hour here for Thee be spent
    In copying our Saviour's life divine.

Then will our hearts from morn to eve rejoice,
    While humbly learning at our Master's feet,
Hearing, obeying then His loving voice,
    Our happiness shall grow in Him complete.

Oh, may we walk so closely, Lord, with Thee,
    That we reflect the brightness of Thy face;
That we may see none beautiful as Thee,
    And long on Thee for aye unveiled to gaze.

Then 'twill be bliss to hear Thy loving call,
    Clasped in Thy safe and tenderest embrace,
And ready-winged we'll mount and leave even all,
    With Thee heaven's golden pavement e'er to pace.

May Thy great glory be our only aim,
  To bring lost wanderers 'neath Thy sheltering wing,
Until in yonder new Jerusalem
  We join the ransomed e'er Thy praise to sing.

By H. A. FEARNLEY.

A FEW LINES IN REMEMBRANCE OF THE PAST YEAR'S MERCIES.

WHAT blessings hath our God bestowed
  Through all the year that's gone;
What battles hath he helped us fight,
  What victories grace hath won.
Amazing hath His watchfulness
  O'er all His people been,
We have not had to pass alone
  The bright or shadowy scene.

Oh often on the darkest path
  His love in radiant light
Burst forth anew, exceeding faith,
  And charmed our wondering sight.
Thus 'mid our tears we should rejoice
  In His great love and power,
Who leadeth all who trust in Him
  To the triumphant hour.

Oh may we do or wait His will,
  Whose love and skill divine
Here and through all eternity
  Undimmed shall ever shine.
May strong unyielding faith be ours,
  Then shall the victory be
Won, while undaunted hope shines bright
  With immortality.

Oh may Thy Holy Spirit, Lord,
  Fill every heart, we pray,
And may our steps each coming year
  Come nearer brighter day.
Oh may we daily grow in grace,
  In wisdom and in love ;
Thus may we daily, while on earth,
  Grow ripe for courts above.

Help us to live that every eve
  May find us nearer Heaven,
Forgiven, while we e'er forgive,
  Thus shall Thy smile be given.
So may we lead some weary soul,
  By footprints left behind,
Safe through the storm to Heaven's fair goal,
  Sweet joy and rest to find.

                    By H. A. FEARNLEY.
January 7th, 1894.

Text—" Thy Will be done."

GOD is all-wise in what He chose
  His child shall do or suffer here ;
Let not my ignorance abuse
  His love or think it insincere.

While I am called to do His will,
  The strength He surely will supply ;
Or if awhile I suffer, still
  In tender arms I e'er may lie.

He doth not will His own loved child
  Should know one grief or tear too much ;
But He would see me undefiled,
  And soon would have me dwell with such.

His justice is too noble, grand,
   To appoint me trials too severe ;
As gold must be by fire refined,
   So He refines and moulds me here.

The flame shall not His loved one mar,
   He never leaves, but watcheth me ;
Soon as His image I shall bear,
   His love in all things I shall see.

When from the furnace heat set free,
   My joy and triumph shall be more ;
While love reveals the mystery
   To me, when perfected and pure.

Ah ! fear not ; His pure love supreme
   Will never let thee suffer pain
More than almighty skill doth deem
   Needful to bring thee endless gain.

Behold Him here, though God divine,
   In deep humility for sin ;
Sin not His own, but ah ! 'twas mine,
   To bring a glorious pardon in.

He came from highest throne of bliss
   Down to the darkest depths of woe
To fill our souls with light and peace,
   That we His wondrous love might know.

And can my loving Lord divine
   Decree His children aught but good ;
Whose love doth most resplendent shine,
   Who e'en for me did shed his blood ?

His power, love, wisdom, soon shall shine
   More bright than gems of highest praise,
When we explore the wealthy mine,
   Its treasures rich, which crown our days.

Then will we render God His own,
　　When He disperses all life's haze ;
Cast at His feet our golden crown,
　　And praise in wonder and amaze.

By H. A. FEARNLEY.

HOPE IS THE STAR OF LIGHT.

Hope, Heaven's true resplendent gem of light,
　　Guilds e'en the shadowy and darkened sky
With rainbow promises and visions bright,
　　To raise the drooping to fair scenes on high.

Yes, all our lives are lit with golden rays,
　　Heaven's angel whispers, 'mid the dreariest night,
Of God's true love, when led in strangest ways,
　　Who leads His loved ones e'er in paths aright.

Hope nerves me now to climb the mountain height,
　　Tells me that Jesus did the mountain climb,
In holy prayer, to bring me joy and light,
　　And that I might enjoy its scenes sublime.

When I am called to cross some chasm deep,
　　And I am longing for some other way,
Trembling, bewildered, while I stand and weep,
　　Hope casts a bridge across, while yet I pray.

When standing on the verge of dark despair,
　　I hear the sweetest promises of love,
And hope's glad light my soul doth safely bear
　　On strongest wings, where all doth beauty prove.

And when my little barque is tempest-tossed,
　　Around me flashing lurid lightning's glare,
And I, in fear and dread, feel ruined, lost,
　　Hope in my Saviour me doth safely steer.

So when I see my changeful journey's end,
　And I must pass o'er Jordan's billows cold,
Hope doth reveal my ever-present Friend,
　Shows me, wide open, yonder gates of gold.

Thus I shall safely reach my heavenly home,
　Borne safely o'er the swelling tide by Him,
Until the jasper walls enclose, I cease to roam
　For aye, in doubt and gloom, am safe from sin.

Then shall Heaven's mansions with sweet music ring,
　In loving praise, for hope's triumphant rays,
Lit by my Saviour, Conqueror, and King,
　Who 'lumined, crowned with bliss, life's wondrous
　　days.

By H. A. FEARNLEY.

Text—"*All things work together for good to them
that love God.*"

BEHOLD, how wonderful
　Are all the ways of God;
He leads to rich and glorious goal,
　Whether through fire or flood.

His will is ever right,
　His love is all divine :
He wishes with unsullied light
　Each gem of His to shine.

If e'er His love permit
　Us tread the furnace hot :
He who doth guide our tender feet
　Tempers our eartly lot.

For if afflictions deep
　Come in His great design,
He moulds us thus for bliss complete,
　That we like Him may shine.

When we His image bear
  Through patience, faith, and love,
He'll crown our sorrow, toil, and prayer
  By rapturous joy above.

Then let us walk with God
  And firmer grasp His hand,
Although the painful rugged road
  We cannot understand.

While we His footsteps tread,
  His sympathies so deep,
In sweetest comforts raise our head
  And dry the eyes that weep.

He ever leads us on
  To bliss beyond compare,
To an unfading jewelled crown,
  The victor's palm to bear.

            By H. A. FEARNLEY.

*Text—"In the world ye shall have tribulation, but be of good
    cheer, I have overcome the world."*

God bless and guard us all through life,
  And bring us nightly nearer home ;
E'er make us conquerors in the strife,
  Say to our struggling souls, " Well done."

Oh may each conflict make us brave,
  In courage true to face the foe ;
Knowing that Christ His own doth save,
  That trial makes our faith to glow.

For if my soul was ne'er distressed,
  His love and pity, deep and true,
My soul in fulness could not taste,
  Nor here its richest treasures know.

'Tis when His child in danger cries,
  Nigh overwhelmed, nigh to despair,
On wings of love our Father flies
  In tender arms my soul to bear.

The way He leads me e'er is best,
  And cannot fail, while Him I trust,
To lead me on to joy and rest,
  Though 'tis the way I dreaded most.

Behind the cloud His smiling face
  Doth shed a golden light divine ;
When on its beauties faith doth gaze
  His love doth in full lustre shine.

If here awhile we suffer pain,
  Our Saviour bore the cruel thorn ;
'Tis for our souls' eternal gain,
  After sad night comes glorious morn.

Lord, help us e'er to watch and pray
  Till Thou shalt call our souls up higher,
Then shall heaven's clear, unclouded day
  Reveal us burnished, purged by fire.

When Jesus, who the victory won,
  Opens to us the gate of heaven,
And gives to each the fadeless crown,
  The glory shall to him be given.

By H. A. FEARNLEY.

A FEW LINES ON THE SABBATH.

WE praise Thee, Lord, for Thy sweet day of rest,
Though marred with earthly soil, with sin oppressed,
Thou bidst us come, lay down our burdens great,
And find sweet comfort at Thy mercy-seat.

After the week's stern trials we have passed
The Sabbath brings us rich and free repast,
And we go forth with strength and grace renewed,
To strive more nobly, to shine forth for God.

We praise Thee for the Sabbath dawn, whose light
Foreshadows here a dawning far more bright,
Whose sweet unfading radiance once begun
Shall know no shadow, cloud, or setting sun.

There tears from every eye are wiped away;
We'll praise unwearying, then, instead of pray;
With angel choirs our worship then shall be
Sincere and blissful through eternity.

Our Sabbaths breathe sweet fragrance from on high,
Winging our faith beyond life's mystery;
Wafting our barques towards Heaven's sunny clime,
Where all God's jewels in His glory shine.

While walking with our God the Sabbath way,
The clouds disperse and darkness turns to day;
Before His glorious heavenly form divine
The path in wondrous radiancy doth shine.

When the rich sunset gilds the western sky,
We hear Thy whisper draw supremely nigh :
" Lo, I am with thee even to the end,
I am thy true, unchanging, loving friend."

When night's dark mantle hides fair scenes from view
He says, " My hosts encamp around thee now ;
Thou art secure beneath My guardian wings,
Thy God and Saviour and the King of Kings."

Oh may my soul, in safety hushed to rest,
E'er lean upon my Surety's loving breast ;
Still gaining hope and courage for the way,
Till it is finished and Thou call to day.

By H. A. FEARNLEY.

Text—" Father, if it be possible, let this cup pass from me ;
nevertheless, not my will but Thine be done."

FATHER, if it be possible
    This bitter cup now take away ;
If Thou canst train my soul as well
    To mount to Heaven by cloudless ray.

But keep me close by Thy dear side,
    Which way e'er seemeth best to Thee ;
And with Thy child through life abide,
    Whatever be Thy wise decree.

May I Thy great design fulfil,
    And in Thy glorious image shine,
Though I may pass through seeming ill
    To reach the heavenly form divine.

If 'tis not possible to bear
    Full likeness of my Saviour now,
Until I tread a vale of tears
    And feel sharp thorns upon my brow,

Give me the grace that clings to Thee,
    And firmer still that grasps Thine hand,
To press in faith through mystery,
    Knowing that Thou dost understand.

Thou knowest all the way I tread,
    Thy love to me Thou wilt make plain ;
Though now the rugged steep I dread,
    Thou leadest but to joy and gain.

When I have heaven's great bliss attained,
    And stand before Thy dazzling throne,
And all these trials are explained,
    Thy love in all things I shall own.

Oh help me, then, Thy will to do,
  Or patiently to suffer here,
Till I Thy hidden secrets know,
  And see in them but jewels rare.

Oh shelter me 'neath Thy blest wing,
  And keep me e'er from sin and fear,
Until Heaven's rapturous praise I sing,
  And Thou hast dried the last sad tear.

By H. A. FEARNLEY.

THE NEW JERUSALEM.

OH, what is heaven, my Father dear?
  From what I read I think
It must be a vast glorious sphere,
  Where all sweet pleasures drink.

For there all tears are wiped away,
  No pride or envy come;
Sorrow and grief is gone for aye,
  With all sin, doubt, and gloom.

Naught enters the grand pearly gates
  Which loves or makes a lie,
But those who stood life's test, and wait
  Till God doth purify.

Until He hath made pure the gold
  By tribulation's fire,
We cannot its bright scenes behold,
  Or hear the "Come up higher."

O Father, make Thy child complete
  Through Jesu's cleansing blood,
That I may walk the golden street
  And gaze upon my God.

That I may see its jasper walls,
　　And its pure sparkling fount,
Its palaces and mansion halls,
　　And crystal sea so broad.

Oh may I with you, white-robed throng,
　　Heaven's bliss for ever share,
By Jesus led to heights along,
　　Raptures beyond compare.

May I, amid unfading bowers,
　　Shout victory to the Lamb,
And 'mongst its rich and matchless flowers
　　E'er glory in His name.

And when its glories e'er I view
　　Throughout eternal day,
And all life's victories I know,
　　I'll praise instead of pray.

Amongst Thy glittering jewels there
　　Oh may I ever shine,
And Christ's own lovely image bear,
　　Who is all love divine.

　　　　　　　By H. A. FEARNLEY.

Text—" I am the light of the world."

LEAD clearly, Light, while earth's bright charming scenes
　　　　My path surround,
Oh may I firmly tread Thy steps, whose beams
　　　　Radiant are found ;
Oh may I mark Thy way and ever tread
In it alone, when snares are thickly spread.

Then will Thy mighty skill direct my way,
　　　　Who is all wise,
Thy loving hand shall be my guide and stay,
　　　　Who holds the prize ;

F

Earth's dazzling dreams cannot my soul allure,
For whilst I walk with Thee I am secure.

And if Thou seest fit my faith to try
    A little while,
Hold Thou my hand, though mysteries shroud the sky
    Upon me smile
E'en on the cloud the rainbow bright shall shine,
To seal Thy promise and Thy love divine.

If yet dark chasms must by me be crossed
    E'er I reach home,
Led on by Thee, guarded by angel hosts,
    My feet shall come
Safe to a wealthy place, and surely prove
While following Thee I learn Thy will to love.

Thus shall the last dark river only bear
    My soul to Thee,
Where I in heaven Thy glorious bliss shall share
    Eternally ;
Then when I gaze unveiled upon Thy face,
For all life's path, I'll yield Thee perfect praise.

H. A. FEARNLEY.

THE PRAYER OF THE SYRO-PHENECIAN WOMAN FOR HER CHILD.

Text—" Lord, have mercy upon me."

BEHOLD our Saviour speaking to the crowd,
In wondrous wisdom casting seed abroad,
When pressing forward, 'mongst the people came
A woman full of grief and bitter pain.
In haste she comes, with anguish in her heart,
Trusting her Lord will hear, and take her part.
'Tis for her dear afflicted child she pleads,
As though its own were her most pressing needs.

" Have mercy upon me," she cried, "O Lord,
O heal my child by Thine almighty word."
But, see, the Saviour seemeth not to care
To listen, to the woman's heartfelt prayer.
" It is not meet to take the children's bread
And cast it unto dogs," He calmly said ;
He tested thus the earnest pleader's faith,
Yet, in reply, she only meekly saith,
" The crumbs which fall down at their Master's feet
From off His table, e'en the dogs may eat."
And now compassion fills the Saviour's eyes,
He listens to the faithful pleader's cries.
True love and pity fly the true to aid,
And, " Be it as thou wilt," He kindly said.
The prayer of faith once more the victory won,
The child was healed, the mighty deed was done.
O trusting soul, still thy petitions bring,
Though long thou wait God's time, thou yet shalt sing
Of His almighty love and comfort sweet,
Which thou hast tasted, resting at His feet.
Thy God may test thy faith a little while,
Yet full on thee He'll turn His holy smile,
For faith doth move the hand that holds the key,
And heaven's great storehouse is unlocked for thee :
The trial of thy faith brings heavenly gain,
Though now to thee it seem but loss and pain,
Thy God doth thus make pure, refine the gold,
To bring thee joy, and happiness untold.
His wisdom far exceeds thy trials here,
His love to thee shall yet shine bright and clear,
The Father's hand will not His child distress,
Only to comfort, to give light, and bless.

By H. A. FEARNLEY.

Text—" *Rest in the Lord and wait patiently for Him.*"

WAIT on the Lord, keep on thy way,
Nor chide impatient His delay ;
Assured if thou must wait awhile,
More sweet will be His loving smile.

His will is best, for 'tis all-wise,
His tarrying blessing in disguise,
His love He will reveal to thee,
Yet, in its perfect purity.

If He chastise a few short days,
Thy tears shall yet be turned to praise ;
While walking with thy Lord below,
Thy pathway e'er shall brighter grow.

He'll consecrate thy sorest grief,
The moments of thy pain make brief :
And these shall all work out for thee
Glory throughout eternity.

When stamped with His own seal divine,
Thou, in thy Saviour's likeness shine ;
And 'tis enough, thy Lord doth say,
And bids thee mount to endless day.

Then will thy soul rejoicing rise,
To take with praise the glorious prize ;
And thou shalt see that all thy way
Was lit with mercy's gentlest ray.

By H. A. FEARNLEY.

Text—"God is Love."

O FATHER dear, Thou lovest me,
      Thy love is pure ;
Thine all-wise hand doth hold the key
To all life's joy and mystery ;
      I am secure.

When Thou dost lead through pastures green,
      Mine heart is glad ;
And every form of beauty seen
Reflecteth the most glorious scenes,
      Where none are sad.

But O when the dark vale I tread,
    My faith is tried,
Yet Thou wilt make what most I dread
To beam the brighter joy ahead,
    The waves divide.

While wheresoe'er Thou leadest me,
    Thy hand clasps mine,
Its warmth doth give new life to me,
Thy love in all things I shall see,
    For 'tis divine.

The rainbow light against the cloud
    I e'er shall see ;
And praise, though thunders rumble loud,
And lightnings flash, while yet my God
    Speaks peace to me.

I'll praise Thee for bright hopes that glow
    'Gainst western sky ;
That soon through Jesus I shall know
A richer dawn than e'er below
    Charmed mortal eye.

'Twill end in naught but endless bliss,
    While God is love ;
He knows the way to rest and peace,
The end from the beginning sees,
    What best will prove.

                        By H. A. FEARNLEY.

Text—" *No night shall be in Heaven.*"

OH, what a wondrous happy thought—
    No night shall be in Heaven ;
No earthly dreams, where castles fall,
    No hopes from Edens driven,
No wintry blasts, no storm's fierce howl,
    No parching, withering ray,

No fierce alarms to scare the soul
   But blissful, cloudless day;
No solemn peal of muffled drum,
   To lead the mourner on,
To tell us death once more has come
   And robbed a happy home,
And taken one whom we revered
   Away from our embrace,
One, who for us hath ever cared,
   To his lone resting place.
No widow's heart bowed down with grief,
   No orphan's tears shall flow,
But all enraptured know no strife,
   No more feel dread dark woe;
For God hath wiped away all tears,
   And leads His people on,
To living fountains, where no fears
   Or trials ever come.
No pain e'er racks the throbbing breast,
   No partings there are known,
For God hath given His loved ones rest
   Through His beloved Son.
No breaking heart, no weary feet,
   E'er tread that blissful shore;
For all shall walk the golden street
   Unwearying evermore.
Our God is there our sun and light,
   Who here hath led us on;
Through all our way He led us right
   To victory and home.
Be not afraid although sharp thorns
   Awhile thy paths bestrew,
There yet shall dawn a glorious morn,
   Where laurels wait the true.
Though withered oft lie earth's fair flowers,
   And oft elude our grasp;
There waiteth us unwithering bowers,
   We're in God's loving clasp.
While in His arms e'en loss is gain,
   For His eternal love

By far exceeds all bitter pain,
  We soon its heights may prove.
And then in heaven we shall see
  The wonders of His grace,
And 'neath His smile eternally
  On all heaven's beauties gaze ;
Love's fulness then we all shall prove
  Throughout eternity,
And own that all God's ways are love
  And right was all our way,
Heaven's diadems shall never fall,
  Nor palaces decay ;
Its pleasures shall repay, for all
  Our losses and affray.

By H. A. FEARNLEY.

Text—"All Thy works praise Thee."

FATHER while Thy day is beaming bright
And birds are thrilling nature with delight ;
When flowers by Thee in richest robes are dressed,
May we Thy boundless love see, richest sight !

While we can tread with Thee through scenes sublime,
Oh may our heart in sweetest praises chime ;
And may all beauty but reflect Thy grace,
All brightness shew to us Thy smiling face.

Oh may our souls with all that's fairest vie,
Thy Holy name to adore and glorify ;
Then may we here thy mission e'er fulfil,
Like our dear Saviour choosing Thy blest will.

And if life's fairest roses we would grasp,
Yet Thou forbiddest, now, our eager clasp ;
Oh may we patient, wait the summons given
That bids us come possess a fadeless heaven.

So may we 'mid the loveliest scenes of earth
Be led to see their noblest highest worth ;
May they but lead us rugged paths to climb
With Thee, to higher bliss than knoweth time.

Whil'st thou art with us morning, noon, and night,
Thou mak'st our pathway radiant with Thy light ;
Until we see the glow of western sky,
And know our longed-for brightest dawn is nigh.

Then will we praise untiring Thy great love
Which led in wisdom our weak feet above ;
Then e'er to Thee the victor's palm shall wave,
Who gives all good we e'er have had, or have.

By H. A. FEARNLEY.

PRAISE YE THE LORD.

PRAISE is the essential gift
    Of every thankful heart,
To our dear Lord our hearts we lift,
    Who doth all good impart.

Praise is the incense sweet
    Which reaches Heaven's high throne,
And bringeth from the mercy seat
    Still richer blessings down.

It wreaths bright coronets
    Around our Saviour's brow,
Whose fragrance God doth not forget
    But doth His smile bestow.

We'll praise the perfect love
    Which wore for us the thorn,
And through Thy grace, yet safe above
    With gems Thy crown adorn.

Not with the flowers that fade,
  But highest glory due ;
To Thee who hath our ransom paid
  We'll tune our harps anew.

We realise e'en here
  That Thou true praise dost bless,
And oft doth dry the falling tear
  And givest us joy and rest.

But sweeter far shall rise
  Our praise for aye above,
Each golden crown will be the prize
  Of Thy victorious love.

By H. A. FEARNLEY.

A FEW LINES WRITTEN AS A LITTLE MEMORIAM TO LOVING PARENTS.

DEAR parents, God hath led you
  Truly in wondrous ways ;
Through a long life to old age,
  Through trial on to praise.

'Mid choice and happy hours
  He safe hath led your feet ;
'Mid fragrance and bright flowers
  Toward the golden street.

United you have journeyed
  Through many a stormy blast,
And God hath brought you victors,
  To praise for all the past.

And strong through His deliverance
  He made your faith to glow,
In loving trust for future,
  For what you did not know.

For 'twas His hand who led you,
   Who doeth all things well ;
And of His love and mercy
   I've often heard you tell.

Until our Saviour calls you,
   Oh, may your future grow,
More luminous and luring
   'Till you heaven's rapture know.

In Jesu's full salvation,
   Your souls then fully dressed,
When ends this life's probation
   "Twill be but bliss more blest.

Oh, may we tread your footsteps
   Where they have followed Christ,
Until our Father calleth
   Us each to endless life.

And when we meet in heaven
   God's love shall be our theme,
Who all our good hath given,
   And did our souls redeem.

               By H. A. FEARNLEY.

A FEW HUMBLE LINES WRITTEN TO OUR BELOVED QUEEN ON REACHING THE DIAMOND JUBILEE OF HER REIGN, FOR HER PROSPERITY AND OUR NATION'S GOOD.—A PRAYER.

God bless you still, our gracious Queen,
   May every nation be
Praising Him for your lengthened reign
   And your prosperity.

Oh may God's smile upon you rest,
    And may He spare you still ;
Of peace and happiness possessed,
    Through His unfailing skill.

May He direct your realm aright
    In all it takes in hand,
May all its actions shed a light,
    Noble and true and grand.

Kindled by God's most holy love,
    Oh may it richly glow,
And may your subjects ever prove
    Sincere where'er they go.

May Jesu's precious love make bright
    Your home, your palace here,
And hope as His true rainbow light
    Illuminate your sphere.

May England's heroes each be armed
    With Jesu's conquering faith,
By Christ be led, unscared, unharmed,
    Conquerors o'er sin and death.

When God shall call His jewels home,
    And gather in His wheat,
Oh may we hear His glad " Well done "
    And enter bliss complete.

May each the pearly gates of heaven,
    Its jasper walls, behold,
And 'mid the white-robed throng be given
    A fadeless crown of gold.

Oh may we meet in courts above,
    And pace the golden street,
Singing of Jesu's boundless love
    In rapture at His feet.

When life's great mysteries we see,
  We'll own He is all-wise,
That He whose hand doth hold the key
  Led on to matchless joys.

Life's bitterest griefs will vanish then,
  All tears be wiped away ;
When we receive Heaven's diadem,
  We'll praise instead of pray.

Then will life's chain in every link
  Shine bright to our glad eyes,
For God doth lead from sorrows' brink
  Up to eternal joys.

By H. A. FEARNLEY.